Captain Blownaparte
and the Big Ocean Clean up

by Helga Hopkins
Illustrated by David Benham

Published as an eBook in 2021
Paperback edition published in 2021

contact@blownaparte.com

ISBN: 9798503873986

Captain Blownaparte™
and the Big Ocean Clean up

by Helga Hopkins & David Benham

Captain Blownaparte and
the Big Ocean Clean up

Captain Blownaparte and his crew were enjoying a lazy day off. The Captain was polishing his gold coins collection. Sproggie, the Captain's little nephew, and Prosper the clever parrot were enjoying a Wizzy-Woo picture book, while the rest of the crew were playing ball with the dolphins.

Suddenly a very anxious dolphin poked her nose out of the sea. She had terrible news! Captain Purplebeard, an extremely nasty pirate had been throwing loads of rubbish overboard and a poor little baby dolphin had become caught up in it! The dolphins had been unable to free the baby and needed help quickly.

'I'd love to help,' sighed the Captain, 'but we can't breathe under water.' 'Well,' said Prosper, 'I know what to do about that. We can build an underwater ship.' So, under Prosper's instructions Swiss Sepp and the crew built an underwater ship from old barrels and bottles, all safely glued together with Sepp's famous sticky toffee.

When the underwater ship was finished they set off in search of the baby dolphin. They paddled as hard as they could while the dolphins helped to push them along. Then, Pirate Tidy who was the ship's look-out became very upset. 'Just look at all the litter in the sea! When we get back we have to stop all those thoughtless pirates from throwing their rubbish overboard'.

Before long, they reached the trapped baby dolphin, and with one mighty push they freed the baby who was happily reunited with her parents!

When they got back, Pirate Tidy and the dolphins decided that something had to be done to stop the pirates from polluting the sea. 'I don't know what we can do,' grumbled Captain Blownaparte. 'They'll never listen to us. But I'll pay a visit to the pirate tavern and try talking some sense into them.'

Sadly Captain Blownaparte was quite right; Captain Purplebeard and his nasty pirate friends had no intention of changing their naughty ways. 'I'll throw as much rubbish into the sea as I want to!' shouted Purplebeard. 'I couldn't care less about the baby dolphins!'

A very angry Captain Blownaparte had to tell the crew that his visit had not been successful. 'I wish we could pile all the rubbish up on the nasty pirates' ships, they wouldn't like that one bit!' said Sproggie. 'It's no good,' sighed Pirate Tidy, 'they'd just throw it back into the sea again.' Then Prosper suddenly started giggling, 'Why don't we stick the rubbish to their ships with Swiss Sepp's sticky toffee, so they won't be able to throw it overboard again!'

Several of Captain Blownaparte's old friends heard of the plan and offered to help. Wilma Whale arrived, followed by Dodgy the octopus, and even Silvertooth the great white shark turned up. Silvertooth whispered to Prosper, 'Why don't I eat all the nasty pirates for you!' But Prosper thought the Captain definitely wouldn't agree with that! 'But let's keep it in mind as plan B', giggled the parrot!

Everybody got busy. The dolphins and their friends collected the rubbish from the bottom of the sea. Rosie and Sproggie were cooking masses of sticky toffee and Swiss Sepp was making a batch of his smelliest cheese. Turnip and his friends were planning to hide the cheese inside the cabins of the nasty pirates to knock them out while all the rubbish was piled on their decks.

Two nights later by the light of the moon, Captain Blownaparte and his friends started 'Operation Rubbish'. Turnip and his mousy cousins quietly placed lumps of Sepp's extremely smelly cheese in the cabins of the nasty pirates. The awful cheesy fumes would definitely send them off into a deep sleep.

Then the dolphins and their friends brought all the litter up from the bottom of the sea, and with a huge swish of her mighty tail fin, Wilma Whale propelled all the debris on top of the pirates' ships. Pedro and Sproggie then poured sticky toffee all over the rubbish sticking it firmly down!

In the morning Turnip and his cousins gobbled up all the stinky cheese and Captain Purplebeard and his crew slowly woke up. 'What's that terrible smell?' thundered Purplebeard. 'I demand that all the crew have a good bath!'

Purplebeard forgot all about the bath when he came up on deck and found mountains of refuse piled high up on his ship. On top of it all was a letter written by Prosper which said: 'All the rubbish you throw into the sea will be returned to you twice over!'

Then Captain Purplebeard saw Muscles trying to pull the sticky mess off the deck. 'Stop that at once!' he screamed, 'We'll have to take all our rubbish to Refuse Island, otherwise we'll be covered in more of the nasty stuff!' And with very angry faces, they quickly sailed off to Refuse Island.

Captain Blownaparte and his friends had been observing from afar and were very pleased with the outcome of their plan. But Silvertooth the shark had a right old grumble at Prosper, 'Such a shame letting them sail away, it's a complete waste of perfectly tasty pirates!'

As usual, they had a big party to celebrate. Some of the crew were swimming with the dolphins and diving with Wilma Whale in the newly cleaned ocean. Swiss Sepp and Pirate Tidy were preparing a great feast. Needless to say, Captain Blownaparte and Prosper were busy reading The Gold & Treasure News in search of more adventures!

Captain Blownaparte's Crew

Pedro   Rosie   Capt Blownaparte   Sproggy   Spike   Pirate Tidy   Alfredo

Prosper

Captain Purplebeard's Crew

Scratch   Scowler   Gertie   Capt Purplebeard   Titch   Muscles   Grumps

Made in the USA
Middletown, DE
10 July 2022

68987916R00022